My Uncle Gus the
GARDEN
GNOME

Jackie French

illustrated by

Stephen Michael King

Angus&Robertson
An imprint of HarperCollins*Publishers*

Angus&Robertson

An imprint of HarperCollins*Publishers*, Australia

First published in Australia in 2004
by HarperCollins*Publishers* Pty Limited
ABN 36 009 913 517
A member of the HarperCollins*Publishers* (Australia) Pty Limited Group
www. harpercollins.com.au

HarperCollins*Publishers*

25 Ryde Road, Pymble, Sydney, NSW 2073, Australia
31 View Road, Glenfield, Auckland 10, New Zealand
77–85 Fulham Palace Road, London W6 8JB, United Kingdom
2 Bloor Street East, 20th floor, Toronto, Ontario M4W 1A8, Canada
10 East 53rd Street, New York NY 10022, USA

National Library of Australia Cataloguing-in-Publication data:

French, Jackie.
　My uncle Gus the garden gnome.
　ISBN 0 207 19958 2.
　1. Family – Juvenile fiction. I. King, Stephen Michael.
　II. Title (Series: French, Jackie, Wacky families; no. 4.).
A823.3

Cover and internal illustrations and design by Stephen Michael King
Typeset in Berkeley Book
Printed and bound in Australia by Griffin Press on 60gsm Bulky white

7 6 5 4 3 2　　04 05 06 07 08

To everyone at Denistone East Public
School — there are no mad scientist or
vampire teachers, but it's a joy of a school.
JF

For Lore
SMK

Chapter 1

The Bad Luck Spell

It was an ordinary day.

Outside the classroom the broomsticks, flying horses and tame dragons hovered above the basketball court as mums arrived to pick up their kids. There was Grizella's magic carpet too, with her genie chauffeur, carefully steering the carpet between the dragon droppings.

Tom glanced up at the clock imp sitting on the top shelf. It held up a sign that read, 'Hold on kid, only ten minutes more and the bell will go!' Tom grinned. He liked school, but he liked knock-off time better.

'Now!' gurgled Dr Maniac, pointing to the diagram on the blackboard with a cackle of insane laughter. 'If we put a donkey brain into a mouse, what do we get?'

Grizella put up her hand.

'Yes, Grizella?'

'A heck of a mess, sir,' she said smugly, tossing her long blonde hair and glancing over at Tom, hoping he'd noticed.

'Quite right, Grizella!' Dr Maniac gave another burst of insane laughter.

Sometimes Tom wondered what it would be like to have a witch or an ogre for a teacher, instead of a mad scientist. Uncle Gus had explained that mad scientists *had* to laugh insanely — mad laughter was one of the first things mad scientists studied at uni.

'The first rule when swapping brains from one animal to another is to make sure they are the same size!' shrieked Dr Maniac happily. 'Now your homework tonight is to find out what sort of brain we *can* put into a mouse's head, without getting bits of brain and clots of blood all over the place! Class dismissed!'

With a final shriek of laughter, Dr Maniac charged out of the classroom, his blood-stained white coat flapping at his heels.

Free! thought Tom happily. He stuffed his books into his school bag and headed out with the other kids. Someone tapped him on the shoulder.

'Hello, Tom,' she cooed.

Tom gritted his teeth. Grizella! He wished Grizella wouldn't flutter her eyelashes at him like that. Life would be just about perfect if it wasn't for Grizella. Okay, she *was* the cleverest girl in the class *and* the richest, and he had to admit she was okay looking too, with her blonde hair and big blue eyes. But ... Grizella's mum was The Most Powerful Witch in the World. The Most Powerful Witch in the World didn't need a good fairy to appear at her kid's christening to ensure her baby was beautiful. The Most Powerful Witch in the World could give her kid anything! Including great looks.

But why did Grizella have to be so keen on *him*!

Grizella gave Tom one of her red-lipped, pearly-teethed smiles. Even her breath smelt like strawberries and chocolate. 'I'm just making sure,' she said sweetly. 'You *are* taking me to the dance on Friday, aren't you Tom?'

'I ... er ... um ...' said Tom.

Grizella's big blue eyes narrowed. 'I've asked around,' she added, not quite so sweetly, 'and you haven't asked any other girl to the dance.'

'I, er ... um ... no,' admitted Tom.

'Then you must be going to ask me!' concluded Grizella confidently.

'I ... er ... um ... n–no,' stammered Tom.

Grizella stared. 'What do you mean, *no*? Don't you think I'm pretty?'

'Er … yes,' said Tom.

'Of course I'm pretty! I'm the most beautiful girl in the school! So my genie will be round at six o'clock to pick you up on my magic carpet.'

'Er … No!' said Tom, hauling his courage up from his ankles. This was really embarrassing! 'I'm not taking you to the dance!'

'What!' Grizella glanced around to see if anyone else was listening, then lowered her voice. 'Why not?' she hissed.

'Because … just because!' said Tom. How would Uncle Gus cope with this, he thought desperately.

'Look, you miserable worm,' muttered Grizella, 'I've told everyone you are taking me to the dance! I'm going to look like dragon droppings if you don't!'

Tom bit his lip. 'I just can't!'

A couple of girls giggled behind them. Tom shut his eyes. It looked like everyone already knew that he'd turned Grizella down.

'You horrible blob of slug vomit!' Tom opened his eyes at the hate in Grizella's voice. 'I'm never going to forgive you for this, Tom Goodle! I'm going to make you pay, you see if I don't!'

'H—how?' whimpered Tom.

Grizella glared at the eavesdropping girls, then looked back at Tom consideringly. 'I'm going to get Mum to put a spell on you! Now what shall it be? Will I get Mum to turn your snot into runny green jelly? No, too obvious. Turn your dinner into puke?' She brightened, 'I know what!'

'What?' asked Tom weakly.

'I'll get her to put a bad luck spell on you!' Grizella threw him an evil grin. 'Everything is going to go wrong for you, Tom Goodle, until you work out that you'd really love to take me to the dance.'

Tom watched her flounce off across the netball court, her blonde curls bouncing on her shoulders, and sit herself defiantly on the magic carpet. He felt the carpet's breeze as it whizzed past him, but Grizella didn't even look his way.

Did Grizella mean it? wondered Tom desperately as he picked up his school bag. Surely even Grizella wouldn't get her mum to put a bad luck spell on someone . . .

Plunk! His school bag fell off its handle, right into a steaming pile of dragon droppings.

Chapter 2

A Mate Named Mog

'Grizella mum, going put spell on you?' someone grunted. Tom looked up. It was Mog, his best friend. Mog was two metres high and covered in fur.

Tom wasn't sure what Mog was. But he was a good mate to have and he was the best football player in the whole school. The other teams just ran away when they saw Mog.

Tom stared at his school bag lying open in the dragon droppings. His books were already turning yellow. 'She might,' said Tom. 'Her mum's The Most Powerful Witch in the World. She gives Grizella everything she wants.'

'Except you, huh?' Mog pointed out.

'Yeah, except me.' Tom bent down and began to pick up his soggy books. 'It looks like my bad luck's already started.'

'Hmmm! No spell on you yet!' Mog bent down to help him.

'I suppose you're right. Grizella hasn't even had time to get home. It must be just coincidence.' Tom stood up, his smelly school bag cradled in his arms. 'Maybe Grizella will forget all about it by the time she gets home.'

'Hhmmmm!' boomed Mog. 'Grizella never forget *nothing*!'

The two boys — well, one boy and whatever Mog was — began to walk down the road to home.

'I just don't understand why Grizella has a crush on me!' said Tom, puzzled.

'Yeah,' grunted Mog. 'You not handsome. You not clever. You got piddling little muscles. You not even play football good.'

'Thanks,' muttered Tom. 'I'm not that bad.'

'Thing me don't understand,' boomed Mog, showing his fangs at a pet gryphon who'd dared to growl at them as they passed. 'Why you not take Grizella to dance? Grizella pretty! And then you safe!'

Tom flushed. 'I want to take Fra,' he said quietly.

Mog's mouth fell open, showing all his big teeth. No one in the school had as many teeth as Mog, or such big ones either. 'You can't take Fra to dance!' Mog boomed. 'Fra not even go to school! Fra a . . .'

'I don't care what Fra is!' interrupted Tom. 'If I can't take Fra to the dance I'm not taking anyone!'

Mog was silent for a moment. 'Fra nice,' he admitted at last.

8

'She's *really* nice,' said Tom. 'And she loves dancing more than anything in the world.'

'Yes, but ...' boomed Mog. He stopped, and shook his furry head. 'You *know* what Fra is! No way Fra can go to dance!'

'I know,' said Tom sadly. He stuck his chin out. 'But if I can't take Fra there's no way I'm going to take Grizella!'

'Hmmm! Then you get heap bad luck,' growled Mog.

CHAPTER 3

TOM'S Uncle Gus

The boys — well, one boy and
Mog — walked along silently.

'Hey,' boomed Mog suddenly.
'There your Uncle Gus!'

Tom nodded. 'Uncle Gus always works in the
Henderson's garden on Tuesdays. Hi ya, Uncle Gus!'

Uncle Gus put down his fishing rod, straightened his
little peaked cap and grinned. 'Hi, Tom! Hi, Mog!' he
called.

Uncle Gus always wore the traditional garden gnome
costume of little red jacket, baggy blue trousers and long
yellow slippers. It might have looked odd on some people,

thought Tom. But the costume suited Uncle Gus's chubby knees and cheery smile.

Sometimes Tom thought it would be great to be a garden gnome too when he left school, with nothing to do except sit in people's gardens with your fishing rod and use a little trickle of magic to keep away the slugs or blowflies. But Mum and Dad were more ambitious for him. They wanted him to go to uni to study warlocking or magic engineering or at least become a headless horseman with his own TV show.

'How was school?' asked Uncle Gus, waving politely to a butterfly who was fluttering through the roses.

'Terrible!' groaned Tom.

Uncle Gus raised a shaggy eyebrow. 'Did Dr Maniac have you making zombie frogs in biology again?'

'Worse!' said Tom. There'd been bits of zombie frog turning up all over the classroom for weeks after that experiment. But Tom would rather have zombie frogs than Grizella.

'Vampire watermelons? Flesh-eating snails?' asked Uncle Gus.

'This real bad,' said Mog. 'Grizella getting her mum put bad luck spell on Tom!'

Tom expected Uncle Gus to look horrified. But he just shook his head. 'Don't worry about it Tom,' he advised.

'Don't worry about it!' cried Tom. 'Why shouldn't I worry about it?'

Uncle Gus smiled. Uncle Gus had the nicest smile in the world, Tom thought. Things always seemed better when Uncle Gus smiled. 'Because it hasn't happened yet! If you kept worrying about everything that *might* happen you'd never have time for happiness at all! Maybe by the time Grizella gets home she'll have changed her mind. Or maybe her mum will say no. Why is Grizella angry with you, anyway?'

'Because I won't take her to the dance,' said Tom. He hesitated. 'I want to take Fra,' he added.

'But Tom . . .' began Uncle Gus.

'I know, I know,' said Tom. 'I can't take Fra to the dance. But . . .'

'I understand,' said Uncle Gus softly. He grinned suddenly. 'You go home and have a really good afternoon tea and enjoy yourself, you hear? And stop worrying about something that might not happen!'

'Thanks Uncle Gus,' said Tom gratefully.

'Hmmmmm, thanks Uncle Gus,' boomed Mog.

'See you tonight, Tom!' added Uncle Gus.

'Yeah, see ya,' said Tom. Uncle Gus had lived with them since Tom was a baby, to help look after Tom because his parents worked at night.

Tom suddenly felt lighter. Somehow things always looked better when Uncle Gus was around. Surely Grizella would change her mind about the spell. And maybe . . . somehow . . . Fra *could* come to the dance.

Tom and Mog continued walking along the footpath.

'Me like your Uncle Gus,' said Mog at last. 'You lucky.'

'Yeah,' said Tom thoughtfully. He *was* lucky. He had a great family and Mog and Fra. What was a bad luck spell compared to that? And there might not even be a spell.

Mog's house was on the corner before Tom's place, next to the gingerbread garage belonging to two old witch mechanics — broomsticks serviced while you wait. Mog's place wasn't exactly a house though, Tom conceded. It was more like a cave, tunnelled into the rock. The garden looked pretty savage as well.

'See you tomorrow,' said Tom, keeping well out of reach of the hungriest looking flower.

Mog punched the flower with his hairy fist before it got too close to Tom. 'Hope so,' he grunted. 'You watch out!'

'I'll be fine,' Tom reassured him. 'I'm sure Grizella's mum won't really put a . . .' he stopped and grabbed his waist.

'What wrong?' demanded Mog, concerned.

'The elastic in my tracksuit pants just snapped!' whispered Tom. 'My pants are about to fall down around my ankles!'

'Hmmm,' muttered Mog. 'Bad luck spell started! You wait, me get you belt!' He grinned suddenly. 'Hmmm! Your underpants have big hole in them! Me can see your . . .'

'Just get the belt, Mog!' urged Tom. 'Please?'

Chapter 4

Bad Luck Begins

No other bad luck happened before Tom got home —
apart from tripping over the gutter and getting gutter
slime down one knee, but that could happen to anyone,
Tom told himself. And being stung by a bee, and having
Kitty-Kat, the sabre-toothed tiger from next door,
growling at him as though she'd been dreaming of Tom
steaks.

But Kitty-Kat growled at him every afternoon. Kitty-
Kat didn't need a bad luck spell to growl at anyone!

Home looked reassuringly normal as Tom turned in the gate. Its four storeys of small windows glinted in the afternoon sun, and above them Fra's high wooden tower reached upwards to the clouds, with bats squeaking round it happily.

Mum had installed the bats last Christmas. She said bats gave the tower a lived-in look.

Tom looked up and gave the tower a wave, just in case Fra was watching (Fra spent a lot of time looking out the window), then climbed the front steps. The door creaked as he opened it.

Mum was in her study checking her lists for that night's work on her laptop. Mum was First Assistant Tooth Fairy. She loved her job, but she found it really difficult keeping track of so many teeth.

'Let's see,' she muttered. 'Fifty-seven teeth, plus little Vampira's front fang and Boo Boo the elephant's left tusk ... Hello, Tom darling. Did you have a good day at school?'

'It was okay,' said Tom. How could he explain Grizella and her spell to Mum? She never understood about him and Fra.

'Much homework?'

'Just a bit about mouse brains. Fra'll help me do it.'

Mum frowned. 'Why not ask Uncle Gus instead? Maybe you're seeing too much of Fra,' she added worriedly. 'I mean, I do like Fra, it's just that ...' her voice trailed off.

'Mum!' exclaimed Tom.

'Oh, all right,' Mum gave in. 'Your dad made chocolate chip muffins,' she added. 'He's in the kitchen putting dinner on. Now, do I take two teeth from Susie Chang or three?' she sighed and peered down at her laptop again. 'Why do people have to get so upset when I get it wrong?'

Tom wandered down the hall. Suddenly in the security of home all his worries seemed silly. Surely Grizella's mum would be too sensible to put a spell on someone, just because he wouldn't take her daughter to the dance, he thought as he opened the kitchen door and . . .

'Hooooooarrrrrowwwwwwwwwwwwwlll!'

Something large and black leapt out from behind the door.

'Hoooooarrrrrowwwwwwwwwwwwwlll!' It grabbed Tom around the shoulders and hugged him hard.

'Hi, Dad,' said Tom.

Dad grinned at him. 'What do you think of my new howl?'

'Cool!' said Tom. 'I bet you get the kids really wetting themselves with that one.'

Dad's grin grew even wider. Dad was Chief Bogeyman for the whole east coast — *no one* was as terrifying as Dad, thought Tom proudly.

He was also the best cook in the universe.

'I made some chocolate chip muffins,' said Dad. 'And it's spaghetti bolognese for dinner.'

'Cool,' said Tom. He loved spaghetti bolognese. 'Look, Dad, there's something I'm a bit worried about.'

'Mm?' said Dad. He peered into the pot of bolognese sauce. 'I wonder if I should add some more basil?'

'It's this girl at school,' said Tom, taking one of the muffins. 'She said she'd get her mum to put this bad luck spell on me. I don't suppose she will really but if she does, we can get someone to take it off, can't we?'

Dad nodded. 'Don't worry kid. If you think she's really done it we can pop down to Dr Whiteskull's surgery before you go to school. Who's been talking about putting a spell on you, anyway? I have a good mind to report them to the principal.'

'It's this girl, Grizella,' said Tom. 'You know, the one who's mum is The Most Powerful Witch in the World.'

Dad stared at him in horror. 'The Most Powerful Witch in the World! Son, there's no way a magic GP can take off The Most Powerful Witch in the World's spell.'

'Oh,' said Tom. 'Who can then?'

'No one,' said Dad flatly. 'Only The Most Powerful Witch in the World can remove a spell once she's put it on you.' He looked at Tom with concern. 'You don't really think she has, do you?'

'I don't think so,' said Tom dubiously. 'The elastic went in my pants and I tripped over the gutter and a bee stung me and my school bag fell into a pile of dragon droppings. But any of those things could have happened to anyone. Right?'

'Of course,' said Dad reassuringly, as Tom bit into his chocolate chip muffin.

'Aarrrrrrgh!!!!' shrieked Tom.

Dad stared. 'Are you practising to be a bogeyman, son? Because I have to tell you, if you're planning to be a bogeyman when you leave school you'll have to howl better than that!'

Tom spat out the piece of muffin. 'Errk,' he groaned. 'Dad, those aren't choc chips in the muffins!'

'They're not?' Dad bent down and picked up the spat out muffin. He looked at it closely. 'Oh, my word!' he whispered.

'What is it?' begged Tom. 'What have I eaten?'

'Bat droppings!' cried Dad. 'I was just sweeping up the bat droppings into a neat pile and I must have mistaken them for the choc chips! I'm so sorry, son!'

That's when the sauce bubbled over.

Chapter 5

Mutant Spaghetti

It took half an hour to clean up the burnt bolognese sauce.

Dad peered into the saucepan. 'I think there's enough sauce left for dinner,' he muttered.

'You don't think it was the bad luck spell, do you, Dad?' asked Tom quaveringly.

'No. No no, of course not, son,' said Dad unconvincingly. 'I'll just heat up the spaghetti in the microwave. You go and set the table.'

Tom had just finished setting out the glasses of moonbeam dew — it was one of the perks of Mum's job — as Dad carried in the big bowl of spaghetti, with almost enough sauce on top of it.

'Grooowllll!' shrieked Dad. (Dad found it difficult to enter a room nowadays without a good bogeyman yell.) 'Dinner's ready!'

'Great,' said Tom. What with everything that had

happened — and the bat-dropping muffins — he was starved. He stared at the dish in front of him.

'Um, Dad?' he began.

'Yes, son? Tuck in,' said Dad, smiling.

'Did you just see the spaghetti move?'

'Move? Spaghetti doesn't move,' said Dad, forking in a big mouthful. 'It just lies there while you shovel it in your mouth.'

Tom looked at the spaghetti suspiciously. 'Dad, I'm sure I saw it move.'

'Nonsense,' said Dad. 'You're just hungry, that's all. Arrrrgggggggh!'

This time Dad's shriek wasn't a bogeyman call. '*Splerrg!*' Dad spluttered, as he spat out his spaghetti. 'It ... it wriggled in my mouth!'

A horrible thought struck Tom. 'Um, Dad, where did you get this spaghetti?'

'From the fridge,' spluttered Dad, staring in horror at the squirming spaghetti. 'It was already cooked in a big plastic container. I just had to heat it up in the microwave.'

'But Dad!' cried Tom. 'That's my term science project! Dr Maniac's been teaching us how to breed mutant worms that are microwave resistant.'

'It's what?' shrieked Dad. 'You mean I nearly swallowed mutant microwave-resistant worms?'

'Well, I nearly ate bat-dropping muffins!' cried Tom.

'Hello, everyone!' said Mum brightly. She was wearing her work clothes: the filmy Tooth Fairy dress spangled with dew drops, the rainbow wings, the belt with the bag of money, and pliers just in case some of the teeth hadn't quite come out.

'Yum, something smells delicious. What's for dinner?' she asked.

'Peanut butter sandwiches,' said Dad shortly, standing up and picking up the bowl of mutant-worm spaghetti to take back to the kitchen.

'But ...' began Mum, then took a look at Dad's face. 'Oh, good,' she said instead. 'Peanut butter sandwiches. Yummy.'

'You don't have to overdo it,' said Dad grumpily. 'Bat droppings, mutant worms, I don't know what this place is coming to ...' Tom heard his dad's angry bogeyman shriek as he entered the kitchen.

'Bat droppings?' enquired Mum.

'Don't ask,' said Tom hastily, as Dad disappeared into the pantry to get the peanut butter. 'Mum, what would you say if I told you someone had put a bad luck spell on me?'

'I'd say, don't be silly,' said Mum comfortingly. 'Sometimes bad luck just happens. Besides, it'd be an incredibly difficult spell. Most spells have to *be* for something, like making your toes drop off or turning princes into frogs if someone kisses them.'

Tom gave a sigh of relief. 'That's what I thought. It was just, well, with the bat droppings and the mutant-worm spaghetti ...'

'No,' continued Mum. 'You'd have to be a *really* powerful witch to make a vague spell like that work successfully. In fact I can only think of one witch around here who'd be powerful enough.'

'Who?' asked Tom. But in his heart he knew the answer already.

'Why, your little friend Grizella's mum,' said Mum. 'I do believe she's powerful enough for any spell. Oh, no!' she gasped, staring down at the tools on her belt.

'What's wrong?' asked Tom. He had a sinking feeling in his tummy, and it wasn't just the bat droppings.

'My pliers are rusty! It was that rainstorm last night — I forgot to dry them! I can't go out with rusty pliers! Someone's sure to notice rust stains on their pillow! And I used the last of the polish a week ago.' She sighed. 'It's just one thing after another tonight!'

Chapter 6

What's Wrong with Everyone?

No one ate much at dinner. Dad was still upset about the mutant spaghetti, Mum was worried about her rusty pliers and Tom was just too nervous to eat.

He could still taste the bat droppings, too.

Finally Mum fluttered down the hallway to her study to get her laptop and GPS navigating device — Mum was no good with maps either. Dad went upstairs to put on his bogeyman mask and his glowing red contact lenses, and his stock of drool to dribble on kid's faces when they woke up and saw him peering over them in their beds. When you were going to terrify kids, Dad always said, you had to do it properly and take pride in your work.

Tom was just putting the plates into the dishwasher when Uncle Gus came in.

Tom brightened. Things always seemed better with Uncle Gus around. 'Hi, Uncle Gus!' he said. 'It's only peanut butter sandwiches for dinner. Dad left you some in the fridge.'

'Hi, Tom. Thank you,' said Uncle Gus gloomily, hanging his little red cap up on the hook by the door.

Tom stared at him. Uncle Gus was *never* gloomy. He was the happiest person Tom had ever met! And he'd been so reassuring this afternoon.

'What's wrong Uncle Gus?' asked Tom. Surely, Tom thought, his bad luck couldn't affect Uncle Gus too! 'Is something wrong at the Henderson's?'

Uncle Gus shook his head, then blew his big red nose into his purple-spotted handkerchief. 'Oh nothing really. Mr Henderson's bad leg is better. Their dog doesn't even lift its leg on the postman now. It's just, well, after you and Mog had gone an old school friend of mine walked by. I hadn't seen him for years.'

'But that's nice!' said Tom encouragingly. 'Seeing old friends is nice.'

'I suppose,' said Uncle Gus, a little sad. 'He's a troll nowadays, did troll studies at uni and now he's in charge of safety and maintenance on that big new bridge. He and his wife have a holiday cottage in Never Never Land and a time-share castle in Fairyland *and* they went snowboarding in Oz last holidays. And here am I ...' Uncle Gus shrugged, and plonked himself down at the kitchen table. 'I just got to thinking ...'

'Thinking what?' insisted Tom.

'What have I done with my life?'

'What's wrong with your life?' asked Tom, surprised by Uncle Gus's question.

'Well, there's your dad — Chief Bogeyman for the entire east coast. And I bet your mum is going to be promoted to Deputy Chief Tooth Fairy as soon as she manages to get her maths right. And you're doing well at school.'

'Not all *that* well,' said Tom,

Uncle Gus ignored him. 'And here I am, nothing more than a garden gnome! You hardly need any magic ability to be a garden gnome! I don't even have my own house!'

'But Uncle Gus!' cried Tom. 'This is your home.'

Uncle Gus looked guilty. He patted Tom's hand. 'I'm happy here, I really am. It's just, well, sometimes I wish I'd achieved just a bit more!'

He heaved himself up from the table. 'I don't want any peanut butter sandwiches,' he said. 'I'll be in the cellar polishing my fishing rod if you need me. It's the Martin's place tomorrow and they do like me to have a shiny fishing rod. Or would you like me to help you with your homework?'

'It's just about mouse brains,' said Tom. 'Fra'll help me.'

Uncle Gus sighed. 'What do I know about mouse brains? I'm not even any help with homework. Have a nice time with Fra, lad. Say hello to her for me. I'll be up to kiss you goodnight.'

Tom listened to Uncle Gus's yellow slippers pitter-patter down the hallway.

What was wrong with everyone? Was it really Grizella's mum's spell? And it was all his fault! Tom bit his lip. He needed to talk to Fra, he decided. Fra could work out any puzzle. She'd know what to do!

Chapter 7

A Word With Fra

Fra lived in the room at the top of the tower. Tom was puffing by the time he'd reached the ninth floor, but it was worth the climb every day to talk to Fra. Outside the tower bats squeaked and whirled, their shadows fluttering against the windows.

Tom knocked on the door of the tower room.

'Come in!'

Tom opened the door. Fra was sitting at the table working on a crossword, her brown hair trailing over her shoulders. Fra loved crosswords. She spent all day just looking out the window or doing crosswords. Other than her table and the two chairs the only other furniture in her tower were bookcases packed with

31

crossword puzzle books and piles of magazines with crossword puzzles.

Mum had offered Fra a bed or a wardrobe or even a vase to put flowers in. But Fra had just shaken her head. What did she need a bed for? Or a wardrobe? Though she'd accepted the vase. Fra loved having flowers in her room.

'Hi, Fra,' said Tom.

'Hi, Tom,' she said. 'What's a seven-letter word for a really nasty person?'

'Grizella,' said Tom, grinning. It always made him feel good just to see Fra. She didn't have blonde hair like Grizella's, and she didn't have blue eyes either. In fact, it was hard to tell what colour Fra's eyes were. They weren't quite green or brown. But she was Fra and that was enough for Tom.

'That's got eight letters,' objected Fra. 'I know! Villain!' She wrote it down then looked back at Tom. 'You look like a vampire's sucked you dry then burped back just enough blood to get you going again,' she observed.

Tom shook his head. 'The only vampire at school is Mr Fang, the sports master. And he only drinks cheetah blood. He says it makes him run faster.'

'Then what's wrong?' asked Fra gently, shoving her crossword puzzle away.

Tom sat down next to her. 'I don't know what to do!' he wailed. 'It's Grizella! She said she was going to get

her mum to put a bad luck spell on me! Then the handle fell off my school bag, and Dad put bat droppings in the muffins and almost ate my mutant worm experiment for dinner. Mum's pliers are rusty and even Uncle Gus is gloomy because he's just a garden gnome.'

'Bat droppings and mutant worms!' gurgled Fra.

'It's not funny!' muttered Tom.

'Yes, it is,' said Fra.

Tom grinned reluctantly. 'Okay, it's a bit funny. But all the rest of it isn't.'

'No, you're right,' said Fra seriously. 'But are you sure it's the spell? Maybe it all, well, you know, happened. Like there are good times and bad times but eventually they cancel each other out.'

'Not so many bad times,' Tom said. 'Not all in a short time. It *must* be the bad luck spell.'

Fra considered. 'Well, can't you ask Grizella's mum to take the spell off?'

Tom shook his head. 'Grizella gets everything she wants. Grizella even has her own magic carpet and genie driver.'

'Then ask Grizella *really* nicely! What did you do to her to make her have a spell put on you, anyway?'

'Nothing,' said Tom sullenly.

'Huh! I bet there was *something*,' said Fra.

'Wasn't!'

'Bet there was too!'

'Wasn't, wasn't, wasn't!' said Tom, grinning.

'Tom Goodle, if you don't tell me what you did I'll tell your dad you borrowed his bogeyman cloak last week to terrify the sabre-tooth next door.'

'You wouldn't!' cried Tom. 'Anyway, Kitty-Kat deserved it! She's always growling at me when I go past.'

'You maggot-brained baboon!' said Fra, glaring at him. 'I'll do anything to help you get out of trouble, Tom. Even if I have to get you into more trouble to do it! So tell me what you did.'

'Oh,' said Tom. He considered a minute. 'You know, I really *like* baboons. Oh, all right,' he bit his lip. 'Grizella wants me to take her to the dance on Friday,' he muttered.

'Well, ask her to the dance then, you ning-nong!' cried Fra.

'No,' said Tom.

'Why not?'

'Because ... because ...'

'Look you silly dunderball!' cried Fra. 'Just ask the girl to the dance!'

'No!' yelled Tom.

'Why not?'

'Because I want to take you!'

Fra sat down again. She was silent for a moment. Tom was horrified to see her wipe a few tears from her eyes. 'I'd love to go to the dance,' she whispered.

'I know,' said Tom softly.

'But I can't.'

'I know,' said Tom again.

Fra hid her face in her hands. 'Sometimes,' she whispered, 'I hate being a ghost.'

Chapter 8

Fra Has a Plan

Fra's real name was The Princess Francesca Mathilda Hermione Arabella Briget Gertrude Elizabeth Emily Alexandra Catherine of Ruritania. And she was 214 years old.

At the same time she was just Fra, and she was Tom's age, because that's how old she'd been when she'd visited her old nurse in this house's tower all those years ago. But the assassins had found her and . . .

Fra wouldn't tell Tom what had happened then. Just that she'd died in this room and become a ghost and she'd been in the tower ever since.

'I wish you could come to the dance,' said Tom sadly.

Fra looked up. 'Me too,' she said dreamily. 'I used to love to dance. I had a ball dress of pink satin trimmed with tiny pearls and roses embroidered around the hem. It was so pretty.'

Tom thought it sounded like total puke. But it also

36

sounded like stuff chicks liked too. Even ghost chicks, he supposed. 'It sounds cool,' he said.

Fra smiled. 'Sometimes I dance up here,' she confessed. 'Not when anyone can see me of course, it would be too embarrassing. You can't really dance properly in a small room, not waltzes and dances like that. But I can pretend ...' her voice trailed off.

'Fra?'

'Yes?' said Fra.

'You could dance for me. I'd like to see you dance.'

Fra took a deep breath. 'No, it's no use wishing for what I can't have,' she said proudly and suddenly she looked like a princess again. 'I'm stuck in this room and that's the end of it! What we really need to think about is your problem!' Fra brightened. 'I know!'

'What?' demanded Tom.

'I've got a plan!' She bent over and whispered in Tom's ear.

It felt weird when Fra whispered so close, thought Tom. Of course you couldn't touch Fra, because she was a ghost. Ghosts could only touch things that didn't live, like chairs and crossword puzzles. But he could still feel the breeze from her whisper against his ear.

Suddenly he realised what she was saying! 'I can't do that!' he protested. 'It's totally yuck!'

'Look, beetle brain,' said Fra, 'I'm a girl, even if I am a ghost and 214 years old, and I know what works with girls! Do you want Grizella's mum to lift this spell or not?'

'Yes,' began Tom, 'but . . .'

'Well then!' said Fra. 'Now, tell me everything that happened at school today!' she ordered.

Tom looked at Fra's eager face. Fra would never go to school, or go surfing or on a picnic. But at least Tom could tell her what it was like.

'First, we had Applied Magic with Miss McUrker . . .' he began.

CHAPTER 9

Kitty-Kat Pays a Visit

It was still dark when Tom awoke next morning. It was stuffy too. Almost, he thought drowsily, as if something hot and furry was sitting on his face.

'Arrrggggghhhh!' screamed Tom, though it came out all muffled. It was hard to scream with a sabre-toothed tiger's bum on your face.

'Grrr?' enquired Kitty-Kat, slobbering gently onto the pillow as Tom leapt out from under her and across the room.

'Help!!' shrieked Tom, trying to spit out Kitty-Kat's tiger hairs. Sabre-toothed tiger bum tasted even worse than bat-dropping muffins. 'Dad! Mum! Uncle Gus! Help!'

'Tom! What is it? I've only just got home!' Dad stumbled tiredly into the room, still wearing his bogey cloak. 'Arrrgggghhh!' he shrieked wearily, too pooped to even bogeyman properly.

'It's Kitty-Kat! From next door!' yelled Tom.

Dad took one look at Kitty-Kat sitting on Tom's bed and another at his son cowering behind the door.

'Don't worry, son!' he cried. 'I'll take care of this!' Dad flashed his bogey cloak in front of the yawning tiger, then took a deep breath.

'Hoooowwwwlllll!' shrieked Dad.

Nothing happened. Kitty-Kat yawned again.

'Er, Dad,' began Tom.

Dad blinked. 'That's odd,' he said, 'everything is terrified of bogeymen.'

'But, Dad . . .'

'Quiet, son. Let me try it again.' Dad took an even deeper breath.

'HHHHHHHHHHHHHOOOOOOOOOOOWWWWW WWWLLLLLLLLLLLLLL!!!!' he shrieked. The mirror on the wardrobe door cracked. Flakes of plaster fell down from the ceiling.

Kitty-Kat lifted a paw and began to wash herself.

MMMMMMOOOOOOOOOOOHHHHHHHHHHHHHHHWWWWWLLLLLLLLLLLLLLL!!!!

'I can't understand it,' muttered Dad.

'It's my fault,' confessed Tom. 'I sort of, er, borrowed your bogey cloak a few times to scare Kitty-Kat. I mean she growls at me from behind the fence on the way home! So I thought I'd scare her and ...' he gulped. 'She just isn't scared of bogeymen anymore.'

'Not scared of bogeymen!' cried Dad. 'Tom, that's the first rule of bogeymanning! Never scare anything too often, or they'll stop being scared!'

Dad shook his head. 'I just hope Head Office doesn't hear about this,' he muttered as he trudged down the hall. 'A bogeyman unable to scare a little pussy cat . . .'

Which left Tom alone with the sabre-toothed tiger.

'Er, nice Kitty-Kat!' said Tom.

Kitty-Kat grinned and showed her fangs.

CHAPTER 10

What's That Smell?

By the time Tom had managed to climb to safety up onto the wardrobe Kitty-Kat had become bored. She squatted on the rug and left a warm yellow puddle over Tom's sneakers, then prowled out the door, waving her tufted tail. Tom watched her pad down the stairs, out the front door, then out the gate and back in the gate next door.

Tom stared. Who'd left the front door open? *And* the front gate? *And* next door's gate too? Or was it . . . ?

Tom gulped. The bad luck spell! He galloped downstairs in his socks to shut the two gates and the front door before Kitty-Kat decided to come back again.

Tom dressed hurriedly and cleaned his teeth twice to get rid of the taste of tiger bum. He poured the tiger wee out of his sneakers and left them on the window sill to dry. The rest of the family were already at the breakfast table when he came down.

Mum looked tired. There was a blood stain on her Tooth Fairy uniform — some kids had forgotten to wash their teeth before they put them under their pillows — and her wings drooped. Dad still looked miffed and Uncle Gus still looked gloomy.

'Hi, everyone!' said Tom, a bit too brightly.

'Hello,' said Uncle Gus, even more gloomily. He bent his head over his porridge.

Tom picked up his spoon. Dad made the best breakfasts. Freshly squeezed orange juice, then porridge with sultanas and . . .

Tom peered more closely at the porridge. They *were*

sultanas, weren't they? Not bat droppings again? Surely Dad couldn't make the same mistake twice, even with a bad luck spell hanging over the house.

No, they really were sultanas. Tom took a mouthful and then another. He was hungry after last night's peanut butter sandwich dinner, not to mention being smothered by a sabre-toothed tiger's bum before breakfast.

After porridge there were scrambled eggs on crispy multigrain toast, then more toast with Dad's special raspberry jam (Tom smelt it before he ate it, but it really *was* raspberry jam, not ink or blood).

When breakfast was finished Mum and Dad went up to bed, to get some sleep for the night's work ahead of them, while Uncle Gus had his second cup of tea. Finally he stretched. 'Well, I'd best be off to work. Don't want to be late. It's old Mrs Martin's day today and she frets about the smallest little thing.' Uncle Gus frowned. 'Well, she used to fret. She's been quite happy lately.' He gave Tom a hug as he passed.

'I'll be off in a minute too,' said Tom, enduring the hug. 'See you tonight, Uncle Gus.'

Tom hauled his old joggers out of the hall cupboard — they were too small but better than damp sneakers that smelt of sabre-toothed tiger's end products. He grabbed his school bag and headed out the door. It had been a great breakfast and nothing had gone wrong!

Maybe Grizella's mum's spell only lasted till midnight, he thought hopefully. No, that couldn't be right, because he'd woken up with Kitty-Kat on his face. Well, maybe the spell lasted only till breakfast time, he tried to convince himself.

There might not even be any more bad luck at all now, thought Tom, feeling his step get lighter, as he shut the garden gate carefully behind him. Well, hopefully not . . .

Tom stopped. He sniffed, then sniffed again.

There was a smell . . .

A sort of cat-like smell . . .

A *big* cat-like smell . . .

Tom looked down at his joggers. One was white and blue. The other one was brown — very brown and squidgy, too — and it stank.

Oh no! thought Tom dismally. He'd trodden in sabre-toothed tiger droppings!

Tom trudged back into the house to clean up.

Chapter 11

Tom Apologises

It was late when Tom got to Mog's place.

'You late,' boomed Mog, slinging his school bag up onto his hairy back.

'Yeah,' grunted Mog's mum, peering out of their cave. 'You very late!'

Mog's mum was even taller than Mog. She was hairier too, and wore a necklace of little skulls around her throat. Tom had never asked whose skulls they were. They *might* be monkey skulls ...

Something screamed in the shrubbery. Tom shivered. He was never sure what animals lurked in Mog's garden.

'You have big good time at school,' grunted Mog's mum, handing Mog a bloody leg of lamb. At least Tom hoped it was a leg of lamb. Mog only ate raw meat, but the school tuck shop refused to serve it, so Mog had to take his own.

'It nice and maggoty,' grunted Mog's mum, nodding at the leg of lamb. 'You eat all up!'

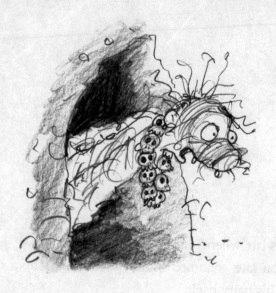

'Yes, Mum,' promised Mog.

'How your bad luck, hmmm?' demanded Mog, as they walked down the street.

'Terrible!' groaned Tom. 'Dad nearly ate my mutant worm project, and now I have to do it all over again. Mum's pliers got rusty, Uncle Gus is gloomy and I was attacked by a sabre-toothed tiger in bed.'

Mog looked Tom up and down. 'You attacked by Kitty-Kat?'

'Well, not attacked exactly. She sat on my face. But it tasted yuck.'

Mog nodded. 'Tiger bum do taste yuck. Leopard bum better. With tomato sauce.'

'Why tomato sauce?'

'You ever taste leopard bum without tomato sauce?'

'No,' said Tom. 'Fra suggested something that might get Grizella to take the spell off,' he added, changing the subject.

Mog listened as Tom told him Fra's plan. Mog shook his furry head. 'Sound like chick stuff.'

'Yeah,' said Tom. 'That's why Fra thinks it'll work. She says Grizella won't be able to resist it.'

'Hmmmmm,' was all Mog said.

The school magic carpet had just dropped its load of kids as Tom and Mog walked through the school gates.

'There Grizella,' whispered Mog, though Mog's whisper was as loud as a volcano at full strength.

Tom nodded. Grizella sat in her usual seat under the paddiewhack tree. (The paddiewhack tree had been a Year 12 magic assignment four years ago. It bore cherries, watermelons and slug and banana sandwiches all at the same time. The slug and banana sandwiches were a mistake — they'd meant to make them toenail and jellybean.)

As usual, a host of boys were gathered around Grizella, trying to pretend they didn't really care if she spoke to them or not.

Tom shook his head. 'I just don't get it! Grizella could go to the dance with any other boy in school.'

'Not me,' rumbled Mog.

'Well, not you,' agreed Tom, tactfully not mentioning that Mog wasn't really a boy. Tom took a deep breath. He really, really wished no one was watching him do this. But it had to be done! 'Wish me luck!' he muttered.

'Good luck,' boomed Mog.

Tom strode over to Grizella's seat. He knelt down beside her, ignoring her glare and reached into his school bag. Yes, here it was . . .

Tom held the bunch of roses and sweet peas out to Grizella. He'd picked them from next door's garden on the way to school. (Luckily Kitty-Kat had been sleeping after her adventure that morning.) *No* girl could resist a bunch of sweet peas, Fra had told him. Tom gazed at Grizella anxiously. Would it work?

Grizella stared at the roses and sweet peas. Then she stared at Tom. Then she gazed at the flowers again.

Grizella smiled. 'They are *soooooo* pretty!' she cooed.

Tom let out a breath of relief. It was working! Now what had Fra told him to say?

'Um ... pray accept these and my most humble apologies!' he recited. It all sounded really yuck to him.

Grizella's smile grew even wider, showing all her cute white teeth. 'Oh, Tom!'

Wow! thought Tom. Maybe Fra was right!

'Um ... do you accept my, um ... heartfelt apologies?' asked Tom anxiously.

'Of course!' cried Grizella, casting a quick look around the playground to make sure that everyone had seen Tom on his knees with the bunch of flowers.

Tom stood up. 'Great!' he said. 'See you in class, Grizella.'

'See you in class,' agreed Grizella. 'The genie will pick you up at six on Friday.'

Tom stopped. 'What genie?' he asked anxiously.

Grizella's smile slipped a bit. 'My genie on the magic carpet who will take us to the dance, stupid,' she snapped.

'But I *can't* take you to the dance!' wailed Tom. 'That's why I apologised!'

Grizella's eyes narrowed. 'Just why can't you take me to the dance, zombie zits?' she snarled.

'Um.' Tom tried to think fast. 'I've got a sore knee,' he said. 'I can't dance at the moment.'

'That's okay,' said Grizella sweetly. 'We don't have to dance.'

'Er ...' Tom's mind worked frantically. Uncle Gus's birthday? He had to take his pet vampire bat to the vet? But Grizella might check to see if he really had a vampire bat ...

'*Please*,' Tom pleaded. 'I'm really, really sorry, Grizella. Please just accept my apology.'

'You know what I think of your apology?' said Grizella sweetly. 'And your flowers?'

'Um, no,' muttered Tom, his mouth dropped.

'Eat sweet peas, buster!' yelled Grizella. She stuffed the flowers into Tom's open mouth and stalked off.

Tom spat out a mouthful of sweet peas just as the school bell rang.

Chapter 12

A Tyrannosaurus Mouse

'So!' Dr Maniac grinned insanely at the class. 'Here is a mouse, yes?' Dr Maniac held it up. It was a very small mouse, all brown and wriggly. 'So what brain do we put in our mouse? Who has done their homework?'

Grizella's hand shot into the air.

'Yes, Grizella?' beamed Dr Maniac.

'A baby rat's brain, sir. Even though rats are bigger than mice a baby rat's brain would fit.'

'Hehehe! Excellent answer,' agreed Dr Maniac with a mad chuckle. 'Who else has a suggestion? Tom?'

Fra had given Tom all sorts of ideas last night. 'How about a lizard brain, sir? Or a snake's brain or a frog's brain?'

'Well done!' chuckled Dr Maniac. 'Hehehe, we will have some fun here! Now, we will try the frog brain first and ...' Dr Maniac blinked. 'Mog? Have you got a suggestion too?'

Tom stared. Mog never had ideas.

'Me ask my mum,' rumbled Mog proudly.

Dr Maniac looked so surprised he forgot to laugh insanely. 'Well, tell us your suggestion, Mog!'

'A tyrannosaurus-rex brain, sir,' boomed Mog.

Grizella snorted. The rest of the class giggled. Tom blushed for his friend.

'I'm sorry, Mog. A tyrannosaurus brain just wouldn't fit ...' began Dr Maniac.

'Yes it do, sir!' objected Mog. 'My mum, she do it.' Mog held up his ten fingers. 'More than that many times! She show me how.'

'But ...' began Dr Maniac.

Mog reached into his desk and drew something out. It was his mum's skull necklace, Tom realised, or one just like it. Mog held it up.

'Oompa ommpa bigga bot,' Mog intoned. 'Make this mouse a bigga lot!'

Zap! The tiny brown mouse fell out of Dr Maniac's hand. As Tom watched it grew bigger, and bigger still.

'That how you fit tyrannosaurus brain into mouse!' said Mog triumphantly. 'Then you get tyrannosaurus brain and ...'

Zap! A wet and slimy tyrannosaurus brain hovered in the air by the giant mouse. *Zap!* The brain disappeared.

The tyrannosaurus mouse blinked. It twitched its whiskers, and then its ears. Then it opened its mouth.

'Groooaaaaar!' roared the mouse.

Tom stared in horror. So did Dr Maniac and the rest of the class.

'Mog!' muttered Tom. 'Turn it back before …'

'Grrrrroooooaaaar!' The tyrannosaurus mouse lunged across the classroom.

Tom blinked. It was heading right for him! He tried to climb under the desk just as the mouse grabbed him in its giant pink-lipped mouth.

'Arrrgh!' screamed Tom, as the mouse lifted him high into the air. 'Mog, do something.'

'Hmmm,' rumbled Mog. 'Mum no tell me how to take brain out.'

'Then … help!' yelled Tom as the tyrannosaurus mouse began to bound over the desks and out into the playground, with Tom dangling from its jaws.

Over the netball court, past the library. 'Gloop! Gloop! Gloop!' cried Tom. He wanted to call 'help' but his mouth was full of mouse dribble. What did the tyrannosaurus mouse plan to do with him? Eat him? Mice liked cheese, didn't they? he thought desperately. But this mouse thought it was a tyrannosaurus! Why me? Tom thought frantically. But deep down he knew. It was the bad luck spell!

Past the hall, down to the oval. The mouse was galloping even faster now. Something thundered behind them. Something that moved like a mountain of legs.

Whump! Something tackled the tyrannosaurus mouse, grabbing it by the hind leg. Something held on as the tyrannosaurus mouse wriggled and squirmed, and twisted round to bite its attacker.

Free! Tom scrambled out as soon as the giant mouth opened. Behind him Mog and the tyrannosaurus mouse struggled on the oval.

Then it was all over. The tyrannosaurus mouse lay still, blinking up at Mog, as Mog stood tall and proud beside it.

'Grolarollarah!!' hollered Mog, triumphantly beating his chest. Then he bent down and grabbed one of the tyrannosaurus mouse's hind legs.

'Better get back to class,' he rumbled.

'I think the class is here!' said Tom, still in shock, gesturing at all the faces staring at them from the sidelines. 'Thank you for rescuing me!'

'My fault,' boomed Mog sadly.

'No, it wasn't,' said Tom. 'That mouse made straight for me! It's Grizella's fault — it's that bad luck spell.' He looked down at the tyrannosaurus mouse, still looking up worshipfully at Mog. 'Um, what are you going to do with the mouse?'

'Him know who boss now,' said Mog confidently. 'Him can wait in class and give us ride home.'

'Eeek!' squeaked the tyrannosaurus mouse adoringly, as Mog dragged it back to the classroom.

CHAPTER 13

Mog Plans a Kidnap

'Me got idea,' said Mog indistinctly, tearing at a maggoty leg of lamb with his giant teeth.

It was lunchtime. The tyrannosaurus mouse was happily rummaging in the garbage bins for scraps to eat, while keeping a sharp eye on Mog in case he had any orders for it.

Tom unwrapped his sandwiches. Cheese and salad, his favourite. 'What idea?' he asked warily.

Mog swallowed his mouthful of meat and maggots. 'We kidnap Grizella.'

'What! You're crazy!'

'Me no crazy,' said Mog reproachfully. 'Me have good idea! We kidnap Grizella, Grizella's mum say, you give Grizella back, I take spell off you.'

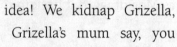

'But we can't go round kidnapping people! It's wrong!' cried Tom.

'Putting spell on people wrong too,' Mog pointed out.

'I don't care! I won't do it!' Tom took a bite of his cheese and salad sandwich. 'Errrrk!' He spat the mouthful out onto the ground.

'What wrong?'

'This isn't cheese and salad! It's soap and salad! Dad's mixed up the yellow cheese with the yellow soap!' Tom tried to spit the rest of the taste out.

'Bad luck spell, hmmm?' said Mog helpfully.

'Yes.' Tom glanced across the playground to where Grizella sat. She looked at the spat out sandwich and smiled nastily, then turned back to her admirers.

'That's it!' roared Tom. The tyrannosaurus mouse looked up to see what the fuss was about. 'I've been sat on by a sabre-toothed tiger, carried off by a tyrannosaurus mouse, had bat droppings in my muffin and soap in my lunch! I've had it!'

Mog grinned. A single maggot wriggled between his giant bloodstained teeth. 'Good,' he rumbled. 'Now we make plan.'

'Eeek!' said the tyrannosaurus mouse, as it scampered over and began to eat Tom's spat out soap and salad sandwich.

Chapter 14

Something Goes Wrong

It was a simple plan.

'Me grab Grizella's genie,' rumbled Mog. 'No genie, magic carpet no fly. You say to Grizella, me walk you home. Me dump genie, grab Grizella as you walk, you do ransom note. Okay?'

'Okay,' said Tom reluctantly. He couldn't get rid of the feeling that this wasn't a good idea. But he had to do something! The bad luck spell was spreading!

The afternoon dragged along. Finally, two minutes before the bell, Mog put up his hand. 'Me need to go dunny, sir,' he said.

Dr Maniac nodded impatiently. 'Off you go then. And take the mouse with you!'

'Yes, sir,' said Mog.

'Eeek!' said the tyrannosaurus mouse. It stopped chewing the leg off Dr Maniac's desk and scampered after Mog.

'So,' said Dr Maniac, 'we have three dead cats. You

take the tail off one, the head off another and the body off the third,' he wriggled his eyebrows in the accepted evil genius fashion. 'We sew them together but we need a lightning strike to make the body come alive. Will this lightning come up from the ground or down from the sky?'

Grizella's hand shot up. 'It depends, sir! Sometimes ...'

Tom counted down under his breath. Five, four, three, two, one ... the bell rang!

'Now for homework tonight,' gurgled Dr Maniac. 'I want an essay on the beauties of a dark and stormy night! Class dismissed!'

Tom ran out of the room and grabbed his school bag. Yes, there was Grizella's magic carpet, lying forlorn by the side of the road. Mog had done it!

Tom lurked by the classroom till he saw Grizella look around for her genie, then sigh and sit on the carpet to wait.

'Hey, Grizella!' called Tom.

Grizella glared at him. 'What do you want?' She smiled nastily. 'Had any good accidents lately?' she added.

'Yes, I have,' said Tom honestly. 'Um, Grizella, as your genie's not around I wonder if you'd like me to walk you home.'

'Why?' said Grizella rudely.

'Well ...' began Tom.

'Because if you think I'm going to change my mind about the bad luck spell you can think again.'

'Um, no, really, I just thought …' stumbled Tom. 'Hey, what's that mouse doing?'

Grizella snorted. 'Stupid mouse. It must be thirsty. It's trying to turn the tap on.'

'It's going to break it if it keeps pushing it like that!' exclaimed Tom, as the frustrated mouse began to pull at the tap with its teeth.

Crack! The mouse hauled the tap out of the ground. *Crunch!* It pulled a length of water pipe, too.

Whooosh! A jet of water speared up into the sky! Higher, higher, higher it fountained! Water cascaded all over the school yard, forming a shallow lake across the netball court then funnelling down towards Tom and Grizella and the magic carpet. Deeper, deeper . . . and deeper still.

There was no time to run. There was no time to do anything! One minute Tom was staring at the wall of water rushing towards him, the next he was swept off his feet in a seething mess of dragon droppings, orange peels and flood!

'Glub!' squawked Tom, trying frantically to get to his feet, to swim across the rush of water, to do anything except sink in the swirling muddy mess.

Something bumped against him. Tom caught a glimpse of the magic carpet, with Grizella still atop, floating past him. He grabbed the carpet's fringe and held on tight, then slowly hauled himself aboard.

Grizella gazed at him with panicked eyes as the carpet bore them down the street on the flood. Tom gazed back at the school. The tap had stopped cascading now. Everyone else seemed fine. It was just his luck that the water had funnelled his way.

Luck, thought Tom dismally. My bad luck . . .

But at least this time his bad luck had caught Grizella too. He glanced at her. She was gripping the sides of the carpet, too terrified even to scream.

At least the water was taking them down the street, thought Tom. The flood hadn't crashed them against anything. Any minute now the water would disperse and leave them stranded or maybe they'd float past Uncle Gus and he would rescue them …

Gurgle, gurgle, gurgle … Tom stared in horror. The water was gushing into the vast black opening of the giant stormwater drain!

They had to leap off! But before he could even finish the thought the carpet plunged into the drain carrying him and Grizella with it.

CHAPTER 15

It Smells Like ...

Darkness, cold and gurgling. The water flowed black on either side. More water must flow into the drain from somewhere else, thought Tom, trying to stop his teeth chattering. There was far more water here than could ever come from the broken pipe at school.

'Tom?' Grizella's voice was small and frightened.

'Yes?' said Tom, trying not to let his voice quaver.

'Where are we headed?'

'I don't know,' said Tom frankly. 'I think the drain flows out to sea.'

'Out to sea!' Grizella was nearly crying now. 'We'll be drowned.'

'Maybe we can jump off at the beach on the way past,' said Tom reassuringly.

'What if we drown before then?' Grizella was crying in earnest now.

Fra wouldn't be crying, thought Tom. He bet Fra

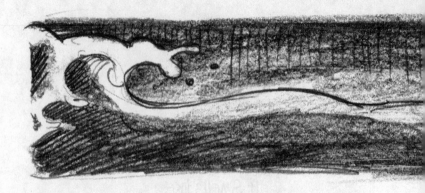

didn't even cry when the assassins grabbed her. Fra would be sitting here planning their escape.

But how could they escape from a magic carpet floating down a stormwater drain? Even if they jumped off the carpet the water would still carry them along.

Maybe if they yelled for help? But who would hear them? And even if someone heard them they'd have floated further away before help came. Maybe … maybe … Tom tried to think.

'Tom,' said Grizella in a small voice.

'Yes,' said Tom. Was she going to apologise to him? Say that if they ever got out of here she'd make her mum take off the bad luck spell?

But all Grizella said was, 'I can see some light.'

'Where?' demanded Tom. But now he could see it too, a tiny pinpoint of yellow in the blackness of the tunnel.

Was it daylight? Somehow it didn't look like daylight.

The light was brighter now. They were getting closer, and closer still. Was this the end of the tunnel? wondered Tom hopefully. Suddenly the drain walls opened out around them.

Tom stared. No, they weren't outside. Instead they were in a wide underground chamber, the daylight filtering in from grates above.

Tom gazed around. Was there anything they could grab and hold on to? But there seemed nothing at all, just the inky water and the slimy walls, and two other smaller channels flowing into theirs.

'Tom?' said Grizella again. 'Can you smell something?'

'Yes,' said Tom hollowly.

'It smells like ...' Grizella tried to find the right word.

It smells like dog doo-doo and puke, thought Tom. It smells like the time the school toilets overflowed on a Sunday and no one discovered the mess till Monday morning. It smells like sabre-toothed tiger droppings, but worse, it smells like ...

'It smells like sewerage,' said Tom. 'I reckon this is where the sewerage tunnel meets the stormwater tunnel.'

'No!' Grizella's anguished cry echoed round the chamber. 'No—o—o, I refuse to float down a sewerage tunnel on a magic carpet! Take me home at once!'

'I can't!' said Tom. 'I can't even get me home, much less you!'

'It's all your fault,' Grizella snivelled.

'My fault!? You're the one who got your mum to cook up a bad luck spell! It's just *your* bad luck that you got caught in my bad luck this time!'

'It is so too your fault!' screamed Grizella. 'If you'd said you would take me to the dance I wouldn't have got Mum to put a spell on you!'

'I don't even understand why you want me to go to the dance with you!' yelled Tom. 'You can have any other boy in the whole school!'

'I don't want them!' sniffed Grizella. 'They just want to go out with me because I'm gorgeous and clever and rich and I can ask my mum for spells for anything! That's all!'

They all sounded pretty good reasons to go out with someone, thought Tom. But all he said was, 'Why me?'

The magic carpet swirled about in a little eddy. It turned round twice then slipped further down the smelly water.

Grizella gave a little gulp. 'Because you're always happy,' she sniffed. 'You're the happiest boy in the whole school.'

Am I? thought Tom. He wasn't very happy now. But had he been happy before the bad luck spell struck?

Maybe it was true, he thought. He *was* always happy. He had a great family, a great friend, Mog, and he had Fra. Mum loved her job as First Assistant Tooth Fairy and Dad was a really dedicated bogeyman. In fact, up until the bad luck spell Uncle Gus had been the happiest garden gnome in the world and all the families he worked for had been happy, too.

Even Fra was happy. Okay, she had been shut in a tower for 214 years, but she made the best of it, and Fra had him too.

Maybe he *was* the happiest boy in the school, thought Tom.

'But aren't you happy?' Tom began. 'You have everything a girl could want!'

But Grizella didn't seem to be listening.

'Tom?' she whispered.

'What?' asked Tom, trying not to look down. Round, brown things were bobbing against the edges of the carpet, but they couldn't be *that*, he thought. Surely the sewerage was treated before it joined the stormwater ... maybe they were chocolates. Yeah, he thought hopefully, some dumb kid had dropped lots of chocolates into the stormwater, maybe the strawberry creams that nobody liked.

'Can you hear something?' asked Grizella, still very scared.

Tom listened. 'It ... it sounds like a roar. A bit like the sabre-toothed tiger from next door.'

'But there aren't any sabre-toothed tigers down here,' said Grizella.

Tom listened again. The roar was louder now. 'Maybe it's a waterfall,' he suggested. Uncle Gus had told him a cool story once about kids who had been washed down a waterfall on a raft and discovered a treasure chest and ...

Grizella shook her head. 'There aren't any waterfalls in a sewerage tunnel!'

Tom supposed there were no treasure chests either.

'Then it's ...' Suddenly, the magic carpet rushed into the tunnel on the other side of the chamber. Darkness washed over them again. But this was a different darkness, with a strange new smell — powerful enough to cover the stink of sewerage.

Faster, faster, faster … it was like sliding down a slippery dip. Except slippery dips weren't dark and slime didn't drip from their roofs, and they didn't roar either.

The roaring got louder, and louder still. The tunnel was getting lighter. There was a glow again in front of them, brighter than before. The brightness grew and grew, till Tom could see the walls of the tunnel, green and slimy, and the ceiling, even slimier.

Then suddenly they were out!

Tom gazed around.

'Oh!' he gasped.

CHAPTER 16

Way Out to Sea

Tom had hoped that the sewerage tunnel went out to sea. That's what Dr Maniac had said it did in Civics class. But while Dr Maniac was pretty good at transplanting mice brains, or explaining how if you had eight zombies and cut each of them up into quarters you'd have thirty-two bits of zombies to sew back together again, he hadn't exactly given the class a lot of detail about sewerage systems.

The sewerage went into the sea, all right. But it didn't dribble out of a tunnel on to the beach, with nice bright sand around it. Well, apart from some sewerage slime and a few brown things.

Tom gulped as the carpet bobbed and swayed in the water. This sewerage pipe went *way* out to sea! All around them was sea — white-topped waves and flying seagulls and just a few bobbing brown things. There was nothing else to see at all, apart from the tunnel, and even that was a sea-coloured, seaweedy green, splashed with waves.

Tom blinked into the distance. Yes, he could just see the land, high brown cliffs with waves crashing at their bases. No nice yellow beach at all.

How long could magic carpets float, he wondered.

'Bother,' said Grizella calmly.

Tom stared at her. 'Bother?' he demanded.

'Yes, bother,' said Grizella. 'My school bag must have got bumped off in the tunnel.' She yawned. 'Never mind. Mum will magic it back for me.'

'Never mind!' yelled Tom. 'We're stuck in the middle of the ocean,' — which was a bit of an exaggeration, but Tom felt it was justified — 'on a magic carpet which is getting soggier and soggier and all you can say is "Bother" and "Never mind"!'

Grizella shrugged. 'What else do you expect me to say?'

Tom blinked. He had expected her to say, *Tom, Tom, save me!*, or even, *Yuck, look at all that smelly brown stuff*, or maybe, *Glerp, I think I'm seasick*. But he didn't think it would be tactful to mention any of those. Instead, he demanded, 'How come you were all trembling inside the tunnel and you're not now?'

'Because we were going so quickly in the tunnel that the genie couldn't find us. But now we're out here,' she shrugged, 'I bet he'll be here to save me within thirty seconds. He'd better or Mum will give him heaps.'

'What do you mean, save *you*?' asked Tom suspiciously. 'Don't you mean, *us*?'

Grizella looked at him pointedly. 'In case you've forgotten, zombie zits, it was *you* who got me into this mess!'

'Me!? It was you!'

Zing!

CHAPTER 17

Back to Grizella's Place

The air flashed pink and purple and a particularly nasty shade of green. Tom grimaced. Uncle Gus said only show-offs did show-off magic.

Zing! The genie appeared in another puff of all-colours-of-the-pencil-box smoke. 'To hear is to obey, oh mistress,' he intoned.

Grizella glared at him. 'What kept you?'

'A giant, nasty, hairy thing, oh mistress,' intoned the genie. 'It grabbed me and carried me away.'

Grizella sniffed. 'A likely story. You wait till Mum hears about this. Now take me home!'

'At once, oh mistress!' agreed the genie.

Tom grabbed the edge of the carpet. He wasn't budging! If they thought they were leaving him in the sea they had another think coming!

The genie settled cross-legged on the front of the carpet. Slowly, slowly, the carpet began to rise above the sea water with the odd brown lump dripping from below, then it moved faster and faster.

Grizella glanced at Tom, as though wondering whether to push him off. She must have thought that being unlucky was enough punishment — or maybe, thought Tom gloomily, she thought there just wouldn't be enough bad luck out at sea. Only sharks, tsunamis, giant octopus . . .

This flying carpet moved faster than any Tom had ever been on. The wind blew through his hair and even most of the sewerage pong blew away. Tom looked down. They were over the cliffs now. There was the school and there was Tom's place, with the bats fluttering around Fra's tower. Tom wondered for a second if the genie might drop him off at home. But he didn't dare suggest it. He was afraid the genie — and Grizella — might take the word 'drop' literally.

Tom had never seen Grizella's house before. No one at school had ever been invited there either. Even

Grizella's birthday parties — fantastic birthday parties with everyone in the school invited — had always been held somewhere else, so they didn't disturb Grizella's mum and her magic.

Once Grizella's mum had magicked up a giant spaceship and sent them all off to a party on the Moon. Well, not the real Moon, conceded Tom, as the party one had been made of green cheese, which tasted pretty good on crackers. He suspected the real Moon would taste pretty yuck. But it had been a great party.

The magic carpet was descending now. Tom gazed down.

Grizella's house was on a mountain, tall and massive above the plain below. There were no roads to it. Tom supposed that guests either came by magic carpet, or were high enough up in the magic world not to need one. Tom gulped. Mum was a great First Assistant Tooth Fairy but Tom doubted whether

she could fly as high as that.
Nor was Grizella's place really
a house. It was a castle, with
straight stone sides and
fearsome towers that made
Fra's tower seem tiny.

Down, down, down
they spiralled. Tom began
to sweat. How was he
going to get out of there?

Chapter 18

The Most Powerful Witch in the World

Zoooom! The magic carpet glided skilfully down on the stone battlements. Grizella scrambled off, without a word of thanks to the genie, who disappeared in another puff of pink and purple smoke.

'Hey!' yelled Tom.

Grizella turned. 'What now?'

'How do I get home?'

Grizella shrugged. 'That's your business! Call a taxi carpet.'

'But no taxi carpet could fly this high!'

'True,' said Grizella. She began to stomp off again.

'Well at least tell me where your front door is!' shouted Tom.

Grizella turned again, and sighed. 'Go down the stairs, then down the next stairs, turn left, down the passage, take the sixth turn right, then left, then left again, go through the Great Hall and the Lesser Hall and the Really Quite Tiny Hall, then down the stairs again and you're at the front door. Then ring the bell for the gorilla to put the drawbridge down.'

'The gorilla?' said Tom weakly.

'Ordinary people have butlers,' said Grizella snootily. 'We have a gorilla.'

'Then what?' demanded Tom.

'Then walk down the mountain. It'll only take you three days or so.'

'No way!' yelled Tom. 'Do you know how worried Mum and Dad and Uncle Gus and Fra will be if I'm not home for three days?'

Grizella glared at him. 'Well, it's all your fault!'

'It's not!'

'Is too!'

'Isn't!'

'What is the meaning of this racket?'

Tom blinked. There had been no tacky pink and purple smoke this time, not even a sonic zoom. Just a sudden very angry witch, her hands on her hips.

The Most Powerful Witch in the World was a short, fat, frumpy woman with thin tight lips, and her hair looked like it had been hacked off with a pair of kindergarten scissors. Tom supposed that when you were The Most Powerful Witch in the World it didn't really matter what you looked like. She wore an ordinary tracksuit, a bit baggy round the knees and bum, with a gravy stain down the front. But there was no doubting that she *was* The Most Powerful Witch in the World.

Grizella suddenly looked nervous. Tom had never seen Grizella look nervous before. She'd been scared in the tunnel, and furious when he said he wouldn't take her to the dance, but she'd never looked nervous.

'Sorry, Mum,' she whispered. 'We didn't mean to make so much noise.'

'Saying sorry doesn't make it any better. You totally ruined my concentration. Have you any idea how much concentration it takes to be The Most Powerful Witch in the World?'

'Er, no,' said Tom.

The Most Powerful Witch in the World looked at him for the first time. 'Who is this?' she demanded. 'No, don't tell me ...' She closed her eyes briefly then opened them again. 'You're Tom Goodle and you are the one who refused to take my daughter to the dance!'

'I ... um. Yes,' said Tom. 'You ... you couldn't take the spell off me could you?' he pleaded.

'Why should I?' she said coolly. 'The daughter of The Most Powerful Witch in the World can have whatever she likes.'

Not *my daughter*, thought Tom, or even *Grizella*. Just *the daughter of The Most Powerful Witch in the World*. He suddenly felt a little sorry for Grizella.

The Most Powerful Witch in the World sighed. 'I have no time for this!' she snapped.

There wasn't even a *zing*, much less coloured smoke. Suddenly Tom tumbled onto the front doormat. He was home! He just had time to catch his breath when his school bag landed . . . on his head.

CHAPTER 19

Uncle Gus's Happy Magic

'So that's what happened,' concluded Tom. He was sitting up in Fra's tower with Fra and Uncle Gus and a big plate of banana sandwiches and a raspberry and pineapple milkshake, too, because Uncle Gus said he'd had a shock and needed to build up his strength.

Fra shook her head, 'I feel sorry for Grizella,' she said. 'Her mum probably has no time for her at all.'

'My Mum and Dad work too,' said Tom.

'But they make time for you! They don't mind you having noisy parties either! And anyway, you have Uncle Gus as well.'

'And you,' said Uncle Gus. He smiled at Fra.

'Well, I found out why Grizella is so keen for me to take her to the dance. She says it's because I'm the happiest kid in school. Or I used to be, anyway,' added Tom, suddenly feeling gloomy again. There'd been half a dead fly in one of his banana sandwiches. He'd eaten the other half before he noticed. It looked like his bad luck was continuing.

'But lots of people are happy!' argued Uncle Gus. 'Every family I work for is happy,' he blinked. 'Though of course they weren't always happy,' he conceded. 'The Ambles were constantly arguing, and Mrs Kafoop's leg used to hurt and Mr Zoranoster was bored all day ... but they're happy now.'

Fra stared at him strangely. 'Say all that again!' she ordered.

Uncle Gus blinked. 'What do you mean?'

'About all the families you work for being happy! They weren't happy once. But now they are!'

'I don't understand ...' began Uncle Gus.

'Don't you see?' cried Fra, clapping her ghostly hands. 'They were unhappy. Then you went to work for them. And now they're happy!'

Uncle Gus stared. 'But I had nothing to do with it! I just stand in the front yard and look decorative. Oh sure, I do a little bit of magic, keep the bird doo off the washing line and the snails off the petunias. But I've never been any good at real magic. Not the sort of powerful magic you need to make people happy!'

'How do you know?' demanded Fra, grinning. 'Some people, like Grizella's mum, are good at all types of magic. But others can only do one sort.'

'Like trolls protecting bridges,' Tom pointed out excitedly. 'And pilots making planes fly, and genies and magic carpets!'

'You see!' cried Fra. 'Your magic talent is to make people happy!'

Uncle Gus blinked. 'Well, goodness me!' He thought about it for a minute. 'Maybe you're right,' he said slowly. 'All my life everyone I've known has been happy. Even at school, I was in the happiest class the teachers had ever known!' A grin slowly spread across

his face. 'I'm not a magic failure!' he yelled. 'I'm not just a garden gnome!'

'No!' cried Tom. 'You're the magicest, greatest garden gnome in the world!'

Fra's greeny-brown eyes gleamed in her shadowy white face. 'You know what this means?' she declared.

'What?' demanded Tom.

'All we have to do is get Uncle Gus to Grizella's and make Grizella and her mum happy. Then Grizella won't need to go to the dance with you and her mum will take off the spell and you won't have bad luck any more!' she ended triumphantly.

'Is that all?' echoed Tom. But he was grinning too.

Fra grinned her ghostly grin back at him. 'Now the first stage of the plan,' she informed him, 'is to get Uncle Gus to school!'

Chapter 20

Uncle Gus Goes to School

'Excuse me?' Uncle Gus's cheery, round face peered through the classroom door.

'Yes?' gurgled Dr Maniac, looking up from the blackboard. 'He he he,' he added.

'My nephew Tom forgot his lunch.' Uncle Gus held out the packet of sandwiches. 'I hope you don't mind my dropping them in to him.'

'Of course not,' gurgled Dr Maniac kindly.

'Thank you!' Uncle Gus beamed. He looked around the classroom. 'Do you mind if I just sit and watch you all for a while? It reminds me of my own happy school days?'

Tom held his breath. Would it work? This was the first part of the plan — to get Uncle Gus sitting in the classroom to make Grizella happy enough to agree to the *next* part of the plan.

But would anyone, even a mad scientist, really believe someone actually wanted to come back to school?

Dr Maniac smiled. And it was a happy smile, thought Tom in amazement, not a mad scientist grimace at all!

'Of course!' gurgled Dr Maniac. 'Stay as long as you like! Now ...' Dr Maniac held up the rabbit they were trying to multiply by four. 'What spell would you use to multiply this rabbit?'

Grizella's hand shot into the air. 'Abra times four cadabra, sir!'

Somehow, thought Tom, even Grizella didn't sound as smug with Uncle Gus in the room.

Suddenly Mog's hand shot up too. 'Me got another answer, sir! Big, better answer!'

'Yes, Mog?' gurgled Dr Maniac.

'You put in another rabbit, sir. They do multiplying for you.'

Dr Maniac stared. His eyes grew wider. Then his mouth opened and he began to laugh.

It wasn't insane laughter this time. It wasn't mad gurgling or even manic giggling. It was just laughter, loud and happy. 'Well done, Mog!' he called. 'That's the best answer I have ever heard! We'll just add another bunny!'

Now the whole class was laughing. They weren't laughing at Mog. They weren't even really laughing at the expression on the rabbit's face. They were just … happy, thought Tom. Really, really happy. And when you thought about it, Tom decided, school was a pretty happy place to be. Or it was today.

The afternoon zapped by, as though someone had put a spell on it. As soon as school finished Tom raced outside. 'Ready?' he hissed.

'Ready,' said Uncle Gus.

'Ready!' boomed Mog, as Grizella walked past them.

'Excuse me, Grizella,' Tom said politely.

'What do you want?' asked Grizella. But she didn't sound as rude as she had yesterday, more like she was curious. She didn't even call him zombie zits.

'I just wondered, well, this is my Uncle Gus. He's a garden gnome.'

'I can see that,' said Grizella with a touch of impatience, glancing at Uncle Gus's little red jacket, baggy blue trousers and long yellow slippers.

'Hello Grizella,' said Uncle Gus kindly.

'Well, Uncle Gus wondered if your mum might employ him. He doesn't have any clients on Fridays and ... and ... could you give us a lift on your magic carpet so that Uncle Gus could ask your mum?'

For a moment Tom thought Grizella was going to snap 'No!' without even thinking about it. But all she said was, 'We don't have a garden.'

'I could sit by your moat and fish,' offered Uncle Gus. 'It's very peaceful to have a gnome fishing in your moat. And I could keep the mosquitoes away, too.'

'My mum keeps mosquitoes away. She's The Most Powerful Witch in the World,' said Grizella.

'I know,' said Uncle Gus, sounding impressed. 'But even The Most Powerful Witch in the World might like to have a part-time garden gnome.'

Grizella hesitated. 'My mum doesn't like to be disturbed,' she said finally.

'I won't disturb her,' said Uncle Gus gently. 'Maybe a part-time garden gnome is just the relaxation she needs.'

'Maybe.' Grizella still sounded doubtful. She bit her lip and thought for a moment. 'All right,' she said at last. 'But if my mum gets angry and turns you both into slugs don't blame me.'

Tom shuddered. But Uncle Gus just looked at Grizella sympathetically. 'We won't blame you, child,' he said quietly. 'If she turns us into slugs, or slimeballs or even warty toads, it won't be your fault. Come on, let's go.'

CHAPTER 21

More Magic Than Meets the Eye

It was even more crowded on the magic carpet this time with Uncle Gus, the genie, Tom and Grizella. The carpet swayed as it took off, and only just cleared the top of the netball hoop before finally zooming up, between the waiting broomsticks and dragons, into the sky.

This definitely was a very powerful magic carpet, thought Tom. But how could you enjoy a ride on a magic carpet when The Most Powerful Witch in the World might turn you into a slug at the end?

Still, it was fun up here, thought Tom. It was impossible not to be happy with the wind in your hair and the dragons gurgling in terror as you zoomed above them. He caught Grizella's eye and grinned at her before he realised what he was doing. To his surprise she grinned back.

'You're lucky!' he yelled above the noise of the wind and the dragons trying to get out of their way. 'Riding home on this every afternoon!'

Grizella's eyes were shining. 'I'd forgotten how much fun it is,' she shouted back. 'You forget to notice when you do things every day!'

Now the mountain was below them, and the castle too. The carpet zoomed down and landed on the stone battlements where it had done the day before.

Zing! The genie vanished in another of his tasteless displays of coloured smoke. The others scrambled to their feet.

Uncle Gus looked around. 'Nice place you have here,' he said, but the clichéd words sounded really sincere. 'It's an incredible view.'

'I suppose it is,' agreed Grizella, as though she'd forgotten to look at the view as well.

'I don't suppose we could see the moat ...' Uncle Gus began, when suddenly without warning, or coloured smoke or zinging noises, The Most Powerful Witch in the World was upon them, staring at them with a stony glare.

'I felt magic,' she said shortly. She looked Uncle Gus up and down, or rather down and down as he was even

shorter than she was. '*Your* magic,' she added looking at Uncle Gus.

'Yes,' said Uncle Gus, 'I apologise for disturbing you. But as you see I'm a garden gnome and I wondered if you may have any need for one? Maybe on Fridays?' he added hopefully.

The Most Powerful Witch in the World snorted. 'Why would I want a garden gnome?' she demanded. 'I can do any garden magic we need around here in between two blinks of an eyelash. Anyway, we don't have a garden.'

'I could dangle my fishing rod in your moat,' said Uncle Gus coaxingly. 'It's very peaceful having a garden gnome around.'

'I don't want ...' began The Most Powerful Witch in the World. Suddenly she stopped and looked at Uncle

Gus more closely. 'There's more magic going on here than I thought,' she said finally. 'Just what sort of a garden gnome *are* you?'

Uncle Gus met her eyes. Then he sighed, 'I should have known we couldn't fool The Most Powerful Witch in the World.'

'No,' said The Most Powerful Witch in the World shortly. 'You can't. Come on. Let's get to the bottom of this.'

CHAPTER 22

A Little Bit of Magic Happiness

All at once the stone battlements vanished. Tom gazed around, half expecting that he and Uncle Gus had been tossed into the castle dungeons, with maybe a torture chamber, or at least rats to bite their toes.

Instead they were in a normal living room. Well, normal if you counted a view across half the world as normal, Tom thought, gazing out the giant window, and with carpet thick as grass and soft as a ghost's whisper.

I wish Fra could see this, he thought suddenly. Fra loves beautiful things. I wish Fra could see something more than the bit of road and houses she can see from the window of her tower.

The sofas were massive, the size of a hippopotamus and just as fat, and there were brilliant paintings on the wall that seemed to change as you looked at them, so you realised they weren't paintings at all, but slices of real life from other worlds.

Suddenly trays of drinks appeared and plates of chocolate chip biscuits hovered in the air beside the sofas. Tom took a choc chip biscuit and bit into it carefully.

They were real chocolate chips too, not bat droppings. He took a deep breath. Maybe everything was going to be all right.

He glanced at Grizella, sitting next to him on the sofa. She looked amazed. 'Mum has *never* done anything like this before!' she whispered. 'She always says visitors are a waste of time.'

'Well?' demanded The Most Powerful Witch in the World. 'Exactly *what* magic are you doing here?' Grizella's mum sounded like she still suspected visitors were a waste of time.

Uncle Gus blushed (the blush clashed with his little red jacket). 'I only realised I was doing extra magic yesterday,' he confessed. 'It was Tom's friend Fra who discovered it. You see, all my life I thought I was the magical dunce of the family. The only magic I was good at was keeping away a few mosquitoes, or earwigs off the roses. But then yesterday I realised — I make people happy.'

The Most Powerful Witch in the World frowned. 'Making people happy is not small magic.'

'I know,' said Uncle Gus humbly. 'But it seems I've been doing it for years without realising.'

The Most Powerful Witch in the World concentrated for a moment. Then she nodded. 'You're quite right,' she said. 'That is exactly what you are

doing. You're magicking a sort of invisible happy smoke all around you. But why do you think we need a happy-making garden gnome?' She glared at him. 'I am quite powerful enough to make us all the happiness we need.'

'Are you?' asked Uncle Gus gently.

The silence grew. It was an uncomfortable silence, thought Tom, as though it might burst if you pricked it with a pin. Then finally The Most Powerful Witch in the World replied in a strange voice, 'What do you mean?'

'Are you happy?' asked Uncle Gus softly. 'Is your daughter happy?'

'Of course she's happy!' snorted The Most Powerful Witch in the World. 'She has everything she could possibly want. She only has to say she'd like something and I magick it up for her. In fact I've programmed a magic spell so she doesn't even have to ask me for small things — she just has to wish for it to happen. That way she doesn't have to interrupt me at my work for trivial things like pet baboons and answers to her homework.'

'Do you have a pet baboon?' whispered Tom, fascinated.

Grizella nodded. She still stared at her mum.

'And you?' asked Uncle Gus, even more softly. 'Are you happy?'

'Me? I don't have time to be happy!' declared The Most Powerful Witch in the World. 'Do you know how much work it takes to *keep* being The Most Powerful Witch in the World? How many upstarts want to take my title from me?'

'Would it be so very, very bad just to be second best? Or even third?' You could hardly hear Uncle Gus's voice at all now.

'I . . .' began The Most Powerful Witch in the World. Then she stopped. 'Do you really think I'd be happier if I were just The Second Most Powerful Witch in the World?' she asked at last.

'I think you might have time to find out how to be happy,' said Uncle Gus.

The Most Powerful Witch in the World gazed at Grizella. 'And my daughter?'

'Sometimes kids need more than pet baboons,' said Uncle Gus.

'Though a pet baboon would be great if there are any spare,' added Tom hopefully. He'd always longed for a pet baboon.

'Very well!' Suddenly The Most Powerful Witch in the World sat up even straighter. 'Let's try being ...' she hesitated, 'happy. We'll see if it works! What do you suggest, Mr Garden Gnome?'

'Well,' said Uncle Gus, 'I usually try fishing.'

CHAPTER 23

A Happy Witch

It was cold on the bum sitting on the stone wall above the castle moat till The Most Powerful Witch in the World magicked up some well-stuffed armchairs that dangled in mid-air above the water. She magicked up fishing lines for all of them, too.

'What about fish?' she demanded of Uncle Gus. 'There are no fish in the moat. Which do you suggest? Piranhas? Baby sharks? Roritanian hairy fish?'

Uncle Gus shook his head.
'You don't need fish to go fishing,' he said. 'We just sit here in the sunlight or the shade if it's a hot day. And we talk a bit and think a bit, then maybe talk again.'

The Most Powerful Witch in the World blinked. 'And *that* makes you happy?'

'Actually just about anything can make you happy,' said Uncle Gus.

'Except eating bat-dropping muffins, or being washed down a sewer with brown bobbing things, or having a sabre-toothed tiger sit on your face,' said Tom.

'Well, most things can make you happy,' corrected Uncle Gus. 'But I like fishing.'

They sat dangling their lines for a while.

'This is silly,' said The Most Powerful Witch in the World. 'A complete waste of time. I haven't bothered fishing since I was a girl. That was with Pop, oh, he was an old wizard then. He'd hold my line as well as his when I got bored with fishing and ran off to play. But when he caught a fish he always said it was my line that had caught it.'

The Most Powerful Witch in the World smiled. 'I haven't thought about Pop for ages. Or Nanna either. Nanna's hobby was breeding polar bears. It was the only magic she was really good at, but you should have seen her with polar bears ...'

The Most Powerful Witch in the World blinked. 'I'm smiling! I'm *happy*,' she breathed. She stared at Uncle Gus. 'It's just your magic,' she accused.

'Well, a bit,' said Uncle Gus. 'But mostly it's just you and happy memories. And making happy memories for your daughter, too.'

The Most Powerful Witch in the World glanced at Grizella. 'Are you happy?' she asked. For the first time she sounded a bit uncertain.

'I am now,' said Grizella quietly. 'It's ... it's not great fun or anything. It's not like skiing down Mt Everest or having my own movie theatre.'

'Hey, wow!' said Tom enviously. He wondered if Grizella might take him skiing on Mt Everest.

'But ... yes,' said Grizella. 'I'm happy.'

'Well!' said The Most Powerful Witch in the World. Then no one else said anything for quite a while. There really wasn't any need.

Chapter 24

Bad Luck is Lifted

'The question really is,' said The Most Powerful Witch in the World, 'why did you come here in the first place? I'm sure it wasn't just to make Grizella and me happy.'

They'd been fishing for an hour. The Most Powerful Witch in the World had magicked up a picnic basket, with muffins that changed to whatever you felt like eating at the time: a mouthful of watermelon and a mouthful of cherries, then a bit of marinated octopus too — Tom loved marinated octopus — and a few potato chips.

All the taste together should have been yuck, but somehow they weren't. Tom thought that when you were The Most Powerful Witch in the World you could magick up anything.

'Well, that's partly true,' said Uncle Gus honestly. 'I thought you and Grizella sounded unhappy. But mostly it was for my nephew here. You see I've helped look after Tom since he was a baby and even if he did spit his stewed pears all over me I've got attached to him. And he was really unhappy because of your bad luck spell.'

'Ah, I see,' said The Most Powerful Witch in the World. 'Well, the spell's off now. I removed it an hour ago.' She shook her head. 'But Tom, I don't understand. Why didn't you just take Grizella to the dance? She's beautiful, she's clever . . .'

'But she's not Fra!' Tom burst out, then flushed. He hadn't meant to mention Fra at all.

Grizella stared at him. 'There's no girl called Fra at school!'

'Fra's a ghost,' mumbled Tom, more embarrassed than he'd ever been before. 'She haunts our tower.'

'But you can't take a ghost to a dance!' cried Grizella.

'I know,' mumbled Tom. 'But it just wouldn't be fair to Fra if I took anyone else.' He blushed even harder. 'Fra's special,' he added. 'And she loves to dance. Fra has so little, and . . .' Tom gulped. There weren't any words for what he wanted to say. Not words that didn't sound soft anyway.

Grizella looked appealingly at her mum. 'Isn't there some way you could make a spell so that Fra could come to the dance?'

Tom stared. 'But you wanted me to take you!'

Grizella blushed as red as Tom. 'Well, it's not like there aren't lots of other boys who'd like to take me. And … and …' she gulped, 'maybe I owe you something,' she added.

But The Most Powerful Witch in the World shook her head. 'There's no amount of magic in the world that can let a ghost go to a dance,' she said. 'Ghosts have to haunt where they were killed. It's one of the basic laws of magic. Even I can't change those. I wish I could help you,' she added.

Tom nodded glumly. 'Thank you, anyway,' he said.

'No!' cried Grizella. 'We can't give up!' Suddenly her eyes gleamed. 'Maybe we don't need magic at all!' she cried. 'I've got an idea.'

CHAPTER 25

The School Dance

The school hall was decorated for the dance. The Art class had pinned up posters on the wall and the Home Science class had made the supper. There were balloons and streamers and fairy lanterns, held up by real fairies who fluttered around the room. Dr Maniac had hung up tiny brains from bits of coloured string, but luckily someone had taken them down again.

It was a wonderful dance.

The leprechaun band was playing up on the stage, their magic guitars pounding out any tune that anyone wanted to hear. And everyone was dancing.

Grizella danced with Mog. She was more beautiful than Tom had ever seen her, with her blonde hair bouncing and her blue eyes alight with happiness. Mog looked pretty happy too. His fur was brushed

for the occasion and he wore a bow tie around his neck, or the bit between his chin and his shoulders anyway, where a neck might be on someone less muscular than Mog.

Tom had never guessed that Mog was keen on Grizella. The things you never guessed about your friends, he thought.

Even The Most Powerful Witch in the World was dancing — with Uncle Gus! Uncle Gus worked Fridays for her now, but somehow he seemed to be spending even more time over there. Tom didn't mind. Uncle Gus had given Tom so much happiness that he deserved to be really happy himself.

Suddenly the music stopped. The dancers wandered over to the sides of the room as the leprechaun band put down their guitars.

The leprechauns picked up violins instead, and violas and a harp. They began to play again, soft graceful music that no one had ever played at a school dance before.

A waltz, thought Tom. Fra had said she loved to waltz.

The hall doors opened and there was Fra. She wore a two-hundred-year-old ball gown, all pearls and satin and a touch of moonbeams too. Tom stepped towards her, almost in a dream.

He took her hand. He couldn't quite feel it, of course. There was no magic that let you feel a ghost's hand. But somehow Tom knew Fra's hand was there.

They began to dance. Tom had never learnt to dance a waltz. But you don't need dancing lessons with The Most Powerful Witch in the World to help.

Round and round the room they twirled. Fra's dress swirled like sunlight, and her face was lit with more than fairy lights as well. Tom thought she had never looked so happy.

Slowly the music drew to a close. The leprechauns took up their guitars again. Fra smiled at Tom as other people began to join them, as the normal school dance music blew out across the hall.

Tom grinned back and touched the bit of wood in his pocket. Yes, he thought, it was still there. It was the bit of wood that let Fra come to the dance, for The Most Powerful Witch in the World was right. Ghosts have to haunt the place where they were killed. But that place doesn't have to stay put.

Tom had sawn round the place on the floor where the assassins had struck at Fra. Wherever that bit of wood went Fra could go too.

Fra was still a ghost, but she was no longer bound to the tower room and a life of crossword puzzles and gazing out of the window. She could go to school now. And she could dance.

CHAPTER 26

Tom and Uncle Gus

It was peaceful in the garden, just the sound of bees in the roses and lizards scuttling through the rocks, Kitty-Kat gnawing at her breakfast next door (Tom hoped it wasn't the postman) and Dad practising a new bogeyman bellow indoors.

'Grroooayooooah!' shrieked Dad. Everything was as it should be.

Tom sat on the mossy rock next to Uncle Gus and watched the goldfish nibble at the worm on the fishing rod. There was no hook on the fishing rod, of course, otherwise the fish might get hurt.

Later, he and Uncle Gus and Fra and Mog would meet Grizella and her mum who was going to take them all on a picnic to one of the moons of Jupiter. The Most Powerful Witch in the World would magick up a perfect picnic place where two kids, a garden gnome, a witch, a ghost, and whatever Mog was, two pet baboons and a sabre-toothed tiger (Kitty-Kat had purred very nicely at Tom ever since Uncle Gus started taking her for walks) would spend a happy afternoon with a basket of magic muffins.

But for now it was just Tom and Uncle Gus.

'Uncle Gus?'

'Yes?' replied Uncle Gus contentedly.

'Can humans and ghosts get married?'

Uncle Gus considered him for a moment. Finally he said, 'No Tom. I'm sorry. You will get older. But Fra will always stay the same.'

'Then . . . then is it a waste of time to love a ghost?'

'No,' said Uncle Gus firmly. 'It's never a waste of time to love anyone.'

'But me and Fra . . .'

Uncle Gus sighed. 'Look Tom, I can't promise you a perfect world when you grow up. No one can. But I can promise you this.'

'What?' asked Tom.

'Things change, if you want them to hard enough. You changed Grizella. You changed her mum.' He smiled. 'You and Fra changed me too. And sometimes ... sometimes the things you want change as you get older.'

'Then there's hope for me and Fra?' asked Tom.

'Of course,' said Uncle Gus. 'Hope is magic too. Come on. We'd better get your baboon ready for the picnic.'

Tom nodded. Suddenly an idea came to him, floating through the air like the sunlight through Fra's dress. Maybe, he thought, maybe Mog and Grizella and me could go back in time. Then we could fight Fra's assassins so she never becomes a ghost! Maybe ...

Tom grinned at Uncle Gus as he began to plan the next adventure. Life was fun!

Other Titles by Jackie French

Wacky Families Series
1. My Dog the Dinosaur • 2. My Mum the Pirate
3. My Dad the Dragon • 4. My Uncle Gus the Garden Gnome
5. My Gran the Gorilla (June 2005)
6. My Uncle Wal the Werewolf (June 2005)

Phredde Series
1. A Phaery named Phredde • 2. Phredde and a Frog Named Bruce
3. Phredde and the Zombie Librarian • 4. Phredde and the Temple of Gloom
5. Phredde and the Leopard-Skin Librarian
6. Phredde and the Purple Pyramid
7. Phredde and the Vampire Footy Team (November 2004)

Outlands Trilogy
In the Blood • Blood Moon • Flesh and Blood

Historical
Somewhere Around the Corner • Dancing with Ben Hall
Soldier on the Hill • Daughter of the Regiment
Hitler's Daughter • Lady Dance
How the Finnegans Saved the Ship • The White Ship
Valley of Gold • Tom Appleby, Convict Boy

Fiction
Rain Stones • Walking the Boundaries
The Secret Beach • Summerland
Beyond the Boundaries • A Wombat Named Bosco
The Book of Unicorns • The Warrior – The Story of a Wombat
Tajore Arkle • Missing You, Love Sara • Dark Wind Blowing
Ride the Wild Wind: The Golden Pony and Other Stories

Non-fiction
Seasons of Content • How the Aliens From Alpha Centauri Invaded My
Maths Class and Turned Me into a Writer
How to Guzzle Your Garden • The Book of Challenges
Stamp, Stomp, Whomp (and other interesting ways to get rid of pests)
The Fascinating History of Your Lunch
Big Burps, Bare Bums and other Bad-Mannered Blunders
To the Moon and Back • Rocket into Reading (September 2004)

Picture Books
Diary of a Wombat • Pete the Sheep (October 2004)

Jackie French

Jackie French's writing career spans 13 years, 39 wombats, 110 books for kids and adults, 15 languages, various awards, radio shows, newspaper and magazine columns, theories of pest and weed ecology and 28 shredded-back doormats. The doormats are the victims of the wombats, who require constant appeasement in the form of carrots, rolled oats and wombat nuts, which is one of the reasons for her prolific output: it pays the carrot bills.

Jackie's most recent awards include the 2000 Children's Book Council Book of the Year Award for Younger Readers for *Hitler's Daughter*, which also won the 2002 UK Wow! Award for the most inspiring children's book of the year; the 2002 Aurealis Award for Younger Readers for *Café on Callisto*; ACT Book of the Year for *In the Blood*; and for *Diary of a Wombat* with Bruce Whatley, the Children's Book Council Honour Book, NSW Koala Award for Best Picture Book, Nielsen Book Data / ABA Book of the Year Award, the Cuffie Award for favourite picture book (USA) and the American Literary Association (ALA) for notable children's book.

Visit Jackie's website

www.jackiefrench.com

or

www.harpercollins.com.au/jackiefrench
for copies of her monthly newsletter

Stephen Michael King

Stephen's first picture book, *The Man Who Loved Boxes*, was nominated for the Crighton award for illustration, was the winner of the inaugural Family Award and was selected for Pick of the List (US). He has since illustrated over 20 books, and has been shortlisted five times for the Children's Book Council Awards. In 2002 he won both the Yabba and Koala children's choice awards for *Pocket Dogs*.

Stephen and his family live on a coastal island in a mud brick house on 10 acres of organic orchards, rainforests and visiting wildlife.

My Mum the PIRATE

Cecil's mum wears long black boots and an even longer sword, and she makes her enemies walk the plank. Putrid Percival serves sea monster soup for dinner, when Cecil would rather eat pizza. Filthy Frederick stinks — but hey, he's good at maths, and nobody's perfect! All Cecil wants is a normal life.

With parent–teacher night looming, Cecil is worried. Will his mum ruin Cecil's newly found street-cred as 'CJ'? But when flood waters strike and Bandicoot Flats Central School is in danger, who will save the students and teachers from the perils of the rising waters? And is Cecil's mum really a pirate?

My Dog the DINOSAUR

Gunk's dad wears fluffy chicken slippers. His sister, Fliss, is into weightlifting and his mum is searching for aliens. Gunk has Spot, his pet dog … or is it? (A dog, that is.)

Spot has a long neck, a flat tail and eats lettuce. Lots of it. Come to think of it, Spot is the silliest-looking dog Gunk has ever seen. Spot is scared of cats, too, and Fliss's motorbike. And then Spot starts to grow …

Will Spot ever learn how to bark? What strange secret does Pete, the girl next door, keep in her shed?

Can Gunk teach Spot to like dog food? Or, will everyone in the world want to take Spot away when they find out that he isn't really a dog?

My DAD the
Dragon

Horace's Dad has silver wings and a green
and orange tail. His mum hasn't been able to
cast a spell right yet, and his sister Grub — the
Fayre Elayne — invents weird things like a box
that can take instant pictures.

At King Arthur's School for Knights the nasty
Sir Sneazle has given Horace the worst
assignment of all. Why couldn't Horace be
asked to rescue a damsel in distress instead of
Pimply Pol, Bran and Snidge, or write an essay
on the broadsword instead of Bernard. Anything
but kill a dragon!

How will Horace and his friends manage?
Will the Fayre Elayne come to the rescue
with one of her inventions? Can Mum cast a
spell that really works? And will Horace
finally discover the truth about his family that
will save Dad and Camelot? Find out as another
hilarious and wild adventure unfolds in the
Wacky Family series.

Watch out for these upcoming
Wacky stories in 2005:

My Gran the Gorilla

My Uncle Wal the Werewolf